Big Sister
and
Little Sister

by Charlotte Zolotow

Pictures by Martha Alexander

HarperTrophy

A Division of HarperCollins*Publishers*

for Barbara Borack

Big Sister and Little Sister
Text copyright © 1966 by Charlotte Zolotow
Illustrations copyright © 1966 by Martha Alexander
All rights reserved. Printed in Mexico.
No part of this book may be used or reproduced
in any manner whatsoever without written permission
except in the case of brief quotations embodied
in critical articles and reviews. For information address
HarperCollins Children's Books, a division of HarperCollins Publishers,
10 East 53rd Street, New York, NY 10022.
Library of Congress Catalog Card Number 66-8268
ISBN 0-06-026925-1. — ISBN 0-06-026926-X (lib. bdg.)
ISBN 0-06-443217-3 (pbk.)

Once there was a big sister and a little sister.

The big sister always took care.
Even when she was jumping rope, she took care
that her little sister stayed on the sidewalk.

When she rode her bike,
she gave her little sister a ride.

When she was walking to school,
she took the little sister's hand and helped her cross the street.

*W*hen they were playing in the fields,
she made sure little sister didn't get lost.

*W*hen they were sewing,
she made sure little sister's needle was threaded
and that little sister held the scissors the right way.

Big sister took care of everything,
and little sister thought there was
nothing big sister couldn't do.

Little sister would sometimes cry,
but big sister always made her stop.
First she'd put her arm around her,
then she'd hold out her handkerchief
and say, "Here, blow."

Big sister knew everything.
"Don't do it like that," she'd say.
"Do it this way."
And little sister did.
Nothing could bother big sister. She knew too much.

But one day little sister wanted to be alone.
She was tired of big sister saying,
"Sit here."
"Go there."
"Do it this way."
"Come along."
And while big sister was getting lemonade and cookies for them,
little sister slipped away,

out of the house,

out of the yard,

down the road,

13

and into the meadow
where daisies and grass hid her.

$\mathcal{P}$retty soon she heard big sister calling,
calling, and calling her.

But she didn't answer.

She heard big sister's voice getting louder when she was close
and fainter when she went the other way,
calling, calling.

$\mathcal{L}$ittle sister leaned back in the daisies.

She thought about lemonade and cookies.

She thought about the book
big sister had promised to read to her.

She thought about big sister saying,
"Sit here."
"Go there."
"Do it this way."
"Come along."

No one told little sister anything now.
The daisies bent back and forth in the sun.
A big bee bumbled by.

17

The weeds scratched under her bare legs.
But she didn't move.
She heard big sister's voice coming back.
It came closer and closer and closer.
And suddenly big sister was so near
little sister could have touched her.

*B*ig sister sat down in the daisies.
She stopped calling.
And she began to cry.

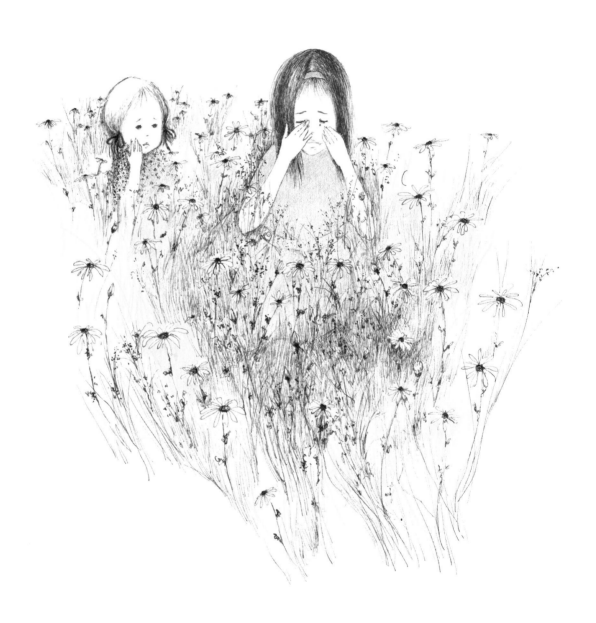

She cried and cried just the way little sister often did.

When the little sister cried, the big one comforted her.
But there was no one to put an arm around big sister.
No one took out a handkerchief and said, "Here, blow."
Big sister just sat there crying alone.

Little sister stood up
but big sister didn't even see her,
she was crying so completely.

Little sister went over and put her arm around big sister.
She took out her handkerchief and said kindly,
"Here, blow."

*B*ig sister did.

Then the little sister hugged her.

"Where have you been?" big sister asked.
"Never mind," said little sister.
"Let's go home and have some lemonade."

*A*nd from that day on
little sister and big sister both took care of each other
because little sister had learned from big sister
and now they both knew how.